I0784680

Fyodor Dostoyevsky

The Crocodile

OK Publishing 2021

Fyodor Dostoyevsky
THE CROCODILE

A Satirical Novella

Published by
MUSAICUM
Books

- Advanced Digital Solutions & High-Quality book Formatting -

musaicumbooks@okpublishing.info

2021 OK Publishing

ISBN 978-80-272-7498-7

Contents

I

On the thirteenth of January of this present year, 1865, at half-past twelve in the day, Elena Ivanovna, the wife of my cultured friend Ivan Matveitch, who is a colleague in the same department, and may be said to be a distant relation of mine, too, expressed the desire to see the crocodile now on view at a fixed charge in the Arcade. As Ivan Matveitch had already in his pocket his ticket for a tour abroad (not so much for the sake of his health as for the improvement of his mind), and was consequently free from his official duties and had nothing whatever to do that morning, he offered no objection to his wife's irresistible fancy, but was positively aflame with curiosity himself.

"A capital idea!" he said, with the utmost satisfaction. "We'll have a look at the crocodile! On the eve of visiting Europe it is as well to acquaint ourselves on the spot with its indigenous inhabitants." And with these words, taking his wife's arm, he set off with her at once for the Arcade. I joined them, as I usually do, being an intimate friend of the family. I have never seen Ivan Matveitch in a more agreeable frame of mind than he was on that memorable morning — how true it is that we know not beforehand the fate that awaits us! On entering the Arcade he was at once full of admiration for the splendours of the building, and when we reached the shop in which the monster lately arrived in Petersburg was being exhibited, he volunteered to pay the quarter-rouble for me to the crocodile owner — a thing which had never happened before. Walking into a little room, we observed that besides the crocodile there were in it parrots of the species known as cockatoo, and also a group of monkeys in a special case in a recess. Near the entrance, along the left wall stood a big tin tank that looked like a bath covered with a thin iron grating, filled with water to the depth of two inches. In this shallow pool was kept a huge crocodile, which lay like a log absolutely motionless and apparently deprived of all its faculties by our damp climate, so inhospitable to foreign visitors. This monster at first aroused no special interest in any one of us.

"So this is the crocodile!" said Elena Ivanovna, with a pathetic cadence of regret. "Why, I thought it was … something different."

Most probably she thought it was made of diamonds. The owner of the crocodile, a German, came out and looked at us with an air of extraordinary pride.

"He has a right to be," Ivan Matveitch whispered to me, "he knows he is the only man in Russia exhibiting a crocodile."

This quite nonsensical observation I ascribe also to the extremely goodhumoured mood which had overtaken Ivan Matveitch, who was on other occasions of rather envious disposition.

"I fancy your crocodile is not alive," said Elena Ivanovna, piqued by the irresponsive stolidity of the proprietor, and addressing him with a charming smile in order to soften his churlishness — a manœuvre so typically feminine.

"Oh, no, madam," the latter replied in broken Russian; and instantly moving the grating half off the tank, he poked the monster's head with a stick.

Then the treacherous monster, to show that it was alive, faintly stirred its paws and tail, raised its snout and emitted something like a prolonged snuffle.

"Come, don't be cross, Karlchen," said the German caressingly, gratified in his vanity.

"How horrid that crocodile is! I am really frightened," Elena Ivanovna twittered, still more coquettishly. "I know I shall dream of him now."

"But he won't bite you if you do dream of him," the German retorted gallantly, and was the first to laugh at his own jest, but none of us responded.

"Come, Semyon Semyonitch," said Elena Ivanovna, addressing me exclusively, "let us go and look at the monkeys. I am awfully fond of monkeys; they are such darlings … and the crocodile is horrid."

"Oh, don't be afraid, my dear!" Ivan Matveitch called after us, gallantly displaying his manly courage to his wife. "This drowsy denison of the realms of the Pharaohs will do us no harm."

And he remained by the tank. What is more, he took his glove and began tickling the crocodile's nose with it, wishing, as he said afterwards, to induce him to snort. The proprietor showed his politeness to a lady by following Elena Ivanovna to the case of monkeys.

So everything was going well, and nothing could have been foreseen. Elena Ivanovna was quite skittish in her raptures over the monkeys, and seemed completely taken up with them. With shrieks of delight she was continually turning to me, as though determined not to notice the proprietor, and kept gushing with laughter at the resemblance she detected between these monkeys and her intimate friends and acquaintances. I, too, was amused, for the resemblance was unmistakable. The German did not know whether to laugh or not, and so at last was reduced to frowning. And it was at that moment that a terrible, I may say unnatural, scream set the room vibrating. Not knowing what to think, for the first moment I stood still, numb with horror, but noticing that Elena Ivanovna was screaming too, I quickly turned round — and what did I behold! I saw — oh, heavens! — I saw the luckless Ivan Matveitch in the terrible jaws of the crocodile, held by them round the waist, lifted horizontally in the air and desperately kicking. Then — one moment, and no trace remained of him. But I must describe it in detail, for I stood all the while motionless, and had time to watch the whole process taking place before me with an attention and interest such as I never remember to have felt before. "What," I thought at that critical moment, "what if all that had happened to me instead of to Ivan Matveitch — how unpleasant it would have been for me!"

But to return to my story. The crocodile began by turning the unhappy Ivan Matveitch in his terrible jaws so that he could swallow his legs first; then bringing up Ivan Matveitch, who kept trying to jump out and clutching at the sides of the tank, sucked him down again as far as his waist. Then bringing him up again, gulped him down, and so again and again. In this way Ivan Matveitch was visibly disappearing before our eyes. At last, with a final gulp, the crocodile swallowed my cultured friend entirely, this time leaving no trace of him. From the outside of the crocodile we could see the protuberances of Ivan Matveitch's figure as he passed down the inside of the monster. I was on the point of screaming again when destiny played another treacherous trick upon us. The crocodile made a tremendous effort, probably oppressed by the magnitude of the object he had swallowed, once more opened his terrible jaws, and with a final hiccup he suddenly let the head of Ivan Matveitch pop out for a second, with an expression of despair on his face. In that brief instant the spectacles dropped off his nose to the bottom of the tank. It seemed as though that despairing countenance had only popped out to cast one last look on the objects around it, to take its last farewell of all earthly pleasures. But it had not time to carry out its intention; the crocodile made another effort, gave a gulp and instantly it vanished again — this time for ever. This appearance and disappearance of a still living human head was so horrible, but at the same — either from its rapidity and unexpectedness or from the dropping of the spectacles — there was something so comic about it that I suddenly quite unexpectedly exploded with laughter. But pulling myself together and realising that to laugh at such a moment was not the thing for an old family friend, I turned at once to Elena Ivanovna and said with a sympathetic air:

"Now it's all over with our friend Ivan Matveitch!"

I cannot even attempt to describe how violent was the agitation of Elena Ivanovna during the whole process. After the first scream she seemed rooted to the spot, and stared at the catastrophe with apparent indifference, though her eyes looked as though they were starting out of her head; then she suddenly went off into a heartrending wail, but I seized her hands. At this instant the proprietor, too, who had at first been also petrified by horror, suddenly clasped his hands and cried, gazing upwards:

"Oh my crocodile! *Oh mein allerliebster Karlchen! Mutter, Mutter, Mutter!* "

A door at the rear of the room opened at this cry, and the *Mutter* , a rosy-cheeked, elderly but dishevelled woman in a cap made her appearance, and rushed with a shriek to her German.

A perfect Bedlam followed. Elena Ivanovna kept shrieking out the same phrase, as though in a frenzy, "Flay him! flay him!" apparently entreating them — probably in a moment of oblivion

— to flay somebody for something. The proprietor and *Mutter* took no notice whatever of either of us; they were both bellowing like calves over the crocodile.

"He did for himself! He will burst himself at once, for he did swallow a *ganz* official!" cried the proprietor.

"*Unser Karlchen, unser allerliebster Karlchen wird sterben* ," howled his wife.

"We are bereaved and without bread!" chimed in the proprietor.

"Flay him! flay him! flay him!" clamoured Elena Ivanovna, clutching at the German's coat.

"He did tease the crocodile. For what did your man tease the crocodile?" cried the German, pulling away from her. "You will if *Karlchen wird* burst, therefore pay, *das war mein Sohn, das war mein einziger Sohn* ."

I must own I was intensely indignant at the sight of such egoism in the German and the cold-heartedness of his dishevelled *Mutter* ; at the same time Elena Ivanovna's reiterated shriek of "Flay him! flay him!" troubled me even more and absorbed at last my whole attention, positively alarming me. I may as well say straight off that I entirely misunderstood this strange exclamation: it seemed to me that Elena Ivanovna had for the moment taken leave of her senses, but nevertheless wishing to avenge the loss of her beloved Ivan Matveitch, was demanding by way of compensation that the crocodile should be severely thrashed, while she was meaning something quite different. Looking round at the door, not without embarrassment, I began to entreat Elena Ivanovna to calm herself, and above all not to use the shocking word "flay." For such a reactionary desire here, in the midst of the Arcade and of the most cultured society, not two paces from the hall where at this very minute Mr. Lavrov was perhaps delivering a public lecture, was not only impossible but unthinkable, and might at any moment bring upon us the hisses of culture and the caricatures of Mr. Stepanov. To my horror I was immediately proved to be correct in my alarmed suspicions: the curtain that divided the crocodile room from the little entry where the quarter-roubles were taken suddenly parted, and in the opening there appeared a figure with moustaches and beard, carrying a cap, with the upper part of its body bent a long way forward, though the feet were scrupulously held beyond the threshold of the crocodile room in order to avoid the necessity of paying the entrance money.

"Such a reactionary desire, madam," said the stranger, trying to avoid falling over in our direction and to remain standing outside the room, "does no credit to your development, and is conditioned by lack of phosphorus in your brain. You will be promptly held up to shame in the *Chronicle of Progress* and in our satirical prints...."

But he could not complete his remarks; the proprietor coming to himself, and seeing with horror that a man was talking in the crocodile room without having paid entrance money, rushed furiously at the progressive stranger and turned him out with a punch from each fist. For a moment both vanished from our sight behind a curtain, and only then I grasped that the whole uproar was about nothing. Elena Ivanovna turned out quite innocent; she had, as I have mentioned already, no idea whatever of subjecting the crocodile to a degrading corporal punishment, and had simply expressed the desire that he should be opened and her husband released from his interior.

"What! You wish that my crocodile be perished!" the proprietor yelled, running in again. "No! let your husband be perished first, before my crocodile!... *Mein Vater* showed crocodile, *mein Grossvater* showed crocodile, *mein Sohn* will show crocodile, and I will show crocodile! All will show crocodile! I am known to *ganz Europa* , and you are not known to *ganz Europa* , and you must pay me a *strafe* !"

"*Ja, ja* ," put in the vindictive German woman, "we shall not let you go. *Strafe* , since Karlchen is burst!"

"And, indeed, it's useless to flay the creature," I added calmly, anxious to get Elena Ivanovna away home as quickly as possible, "as our dear Ivan Matveitch is by now probably soaring somewhere in the empyrean."

"My dear" — we suddenly heard, to our intense amazement, the voice of Ivan Matveitch — "my dear, my advice is to apply direct to the superintendent's office, as without the assistance of the police the German will never be made to see reason."

These words, uttered with firmness and aplomb, and expressing an exceptional presence of mind, for the first minute so astounded us that we could not believe our ears. But, of course, we ran at once to the crocodile's tank, and with equal reverence and incredulity listened to the unhappy captive. His voice was muffled, thin and even squeaky, as though it came from a considerable distance. It reminded one of a jocose person who, covering his mouth with a pillow, shouts from an adjoining room, trying to mimic the sound of two peasants calling to one another in a deserted plain or across a wide ravine — a performance to which I once had the pleasure of listening in a friend's house at Christmas.

"Ivan Matveitch, my dear, and so you are alive!" faltered Elena Ivanovna.

"Alive and well," answered Ivan Matveitch, "and, thanks to the Almighty, swallowed without any damage whatever. I am only uneasy as to the view my superiors may take of the incident; for after getting a permit to go abroad I've got into a crocodile, which seems anything but clever."

"But, my dear, don't trouble your head about being clever; first of all we must somehow excavate you from where you are," Elena Ivanovna interrupted.

"Excavate!" cried the proprietor. "I will not let my crocodile be excavated. Now the *publicum* will come many more, and I will *fünfzig* kopecks ask and Karlchen will cease to burst."

"*Gott sei dank!* " put in his wife.

"They are right," Ivan Matveitch observed tranquilly; "the principles of economics before everything."

"My dear! I will fly at once to the authorities and lodge a complaint, for I feel that we cannot settle this mess by ourselves."

"I think so too," observed Ivan Matveitch; "but in our age of industrial crisis it is not easy to rip open the belly of a crocodile without economic compensation, and meanwhile the inevitable question presents itself: What will the German take for his crocodile? And with it another: How will it be paid? For, as you know, I have no means...."

"Perhaps out of your salary...." I observed timidly, but the proprietor interrupted me at once.

"I will not the crocodile sell; I will for three thousand the crocodile sell! I will for four thousand the crocodile sell! Now the *publicum* will come very many. I will for five thousand the crocodile sell!"

In fact he gave himself insufferable airs. Covetousness and a revolting greed gleamed joyfully in his eyes.

"I am going!" I cried indignantly.

"And I! I too! I shall go to Andrey Osipitch himself. I will soften him with my tears," whined Elena Ivanovna.

"Don't do that, my dear," Ivan Matveitch hastened to interpose. He had long been jealous of Andrey Osipitch on his wife's account, and he knew she would enjoy going to weep before a gentleman of refinement, for tears suited her. "And I don't advise you to do so either, my friend," he added, addressing me. "It's no good plunging headlong in that slap-dash way; there's no knowing what it may lead to. You had much better go to-day to Timofey Semyonitch, as though to pay an ordinary visit; he is an old-fashioned and by no means brilliant man, but he is trustworthy, and what matters most of all, he is straightforward. Give him my greetings and describe the circumstances of the case. And since I owe him seven roubles over our last game of cards, take the opportunity to pay him the money; that will soften the stern old man. In any case his advice may serve as a guide for us. And meanwhile take Elena Ivanovna home.... Calm yourself, my dear," he continued, addressing her. "I am weary of these outcries and feminine squabblings, and should like a nap. It's soft and warm in here, though I have hardly had time to look round in this unexpected haven."

"Look round! Why, is it light in there?" cried Elena Ivanovna in a tone of relief.

"I am surrounded by impenetrable night," answered the poor captive; "but I can feel and, so to speak, have a look round with my hands.... Goodbye; set your mind at rest and don't deny yourself recreation and diversion. Till tomorrow! And you, Semyon Semyonitch, come to me in the evening, and as you are absentminded and may forget it, tie a knot in your handkerchief."

I confess I was glad to get away, for I was overtired and somewhat bored. Hastening to offer my arm to the disconsolate Elena Ivanovna, whose charms were only enhanced by her agitation, I hurriedly led her out of the crocodile room.

"The charge will be another quarter-rouble in the evening," the proprietor called after us.

"Oh, dear, how greedy they are!" said Elena Ivanovna, looking at herself in every mirror on the walls of the Arcade, and evidently aware that she was looking prettier than usual.

"The principles of economics," I answered with some emotion, proud that passersby should see the lady on my arm.

"The principles of economics," she drawled in a touching little voice. "I did not in the least understand what Ivan Matveitch said about those horrid economics just now."

"I will explain to you," I answered, and began at once telling her of the beneficial effects of the introduction of foreign capital into our country, upon which I had read an article in the *Petersburg News* and the *Voice* that morning.

"How strange it is," she interrupted, after listening for some time. "But do leave off, you horrid man. What nonsense you are talking.... Tell me, do I look purple?"

"You look perfect, and not purple!" I observed, seizing the opportunity to pay her a compliment.

"Naughty man!" she said complacently. "Poor Ivan Matveitch," she added a minute later, putting her little head on one side coquettishly. "I am really sorry for him. Oh, dear!" she cried suddenly, "how is he going to have his dinner...and...and...what will he do...if he wants anything?"

"An unforeseen question," I answered, perplexed in my turn. To tell the truth, it had not entered my head, so much more practical are women than we men in the solution of the problems of daily life!

"Poor dear! how could he have got into such a mess...nothing to amuse him, and in the dark.... How vexing it is that I have no photograph of him.... And so now I am a sort of widow," she added, with a seductive smile, evidently interested in her new position. "Hm!...I am sorry for him, though."

It was, in short, the expression of the very natural and intelligible grief of a young and interesting wife for the loss of her husband. I took her home at last, soothed her, and after dining with her and drinking a cup of aromatic coffee, set off at six o'clock to Timofey Semyonitch, calculating that at that hour all married people of settled habits would be sitting or lying down at home.

Having written this first chapter in a style appropriate to the incident recorded, I intend to proceed in a language more natural though less elevated, and I beg to forewarn the reader of the fact.

II

The venerable Timofey Semyonitch met me rather nervously, as though somewhat embarrassed. He led me to his tiny study and shut the door carefully, "that the children may not hinder us," he added with evident uneasiness. There he made me sit down on a chair by the writing-table, sat down himself in an easy chair, wrapped round him the skirts of his old wadded dressing-gown, and assumed an official and even severe air, in readiness for anything, though he was not my chief nor Ivan Matveitch's, and had hitherto been reckoned as a colleague and even a friend.

"First of all," he said, "take note that I am not a person in authority, but just such a subordinate official as you and Ivan Matveitch.... I have nothing to do with it, and do not intend to mix myself up in the affair."

I was surprised to find that he apparently knew all about it already. In spite of that I told him the whole story over in detail. I spoke with positive excitement, for I was at that moment fulfilling the obligations of a true friend. He listened without special surprise, but with evident signs of suspicion.

"Only fancy," he said, "I always believed that this would be sure to happen to him."

"Why, Timofey Semyonitch? It is a very unusual incident in itself...."

"I admit it. But Ivan Matveitch's whole career in the service was leading up to this end. He was flighty — conceited indeed. It was always 'progress' and ideas of all sorts, and this is what progress brings people to!"

"But this is a most unusual incident and cannot possibly serve as a general rule for all progressives."

"Yes, indeed it can. You see, it's the effect of over-education, I assure you. For over-education leads people to poke their noses into all sorts of places, especially where they are not invited. Though perhaps you know best," he added, as though offended. "I am an old man and not of much education. I began as a soldier's son, and this year has been the jubilee of my service."

"Oh, no, Timofey Semyonitch, not at all. On the contrary, Ivan Matveitch is eager for your advice; he is eager for your guidance. He implores it, so to say, with tears."

"So to say, with tears! Hm! Those are crocodile's tears and one cannot quite believe in them. Tell me, what possessed him to want to go abroad? And how could he afford to go? Why, he has no private means!"

"He had saved the money from his last bonus," I answered plaintively. "He only wanted to go for three months — to Switzerland... to the land of William Tell."

"William Tell? Hm!"

"He wanted to meet the spring at Naples, to see the museums, the customs, the animals...."

"Hm! The animals! I think it was simply from pride. What animals? Animals, indeed! Haven't we animals enough? We have museums, menageries, camels. There are bears quite close to Petersburg! And here he's got inside a crocodile himself...."

"Oh, come, Timofey Semyonitch! The man is in trouble, the man appeals to you as to a friend, as to an older relation, craves for advice — and you reproach him. Have pity at least on the unfortunate Elena Ivanovna!"

"You are speaking of his wife? A charming little lady," said Timofey Semyonitch, visibly softening and taking a pinch of snuff with relish. "Particularly prepossessing. And so plump, and always putting her pretty little head on one side.... Very agreeable. Andrey Osipitch was speaking of her only the other day."

"Speaking of her?"

"Yes, and in very flattering terms. Such a bust, he said, such eyes, such hair.... A sugarplum, he said, not a lady — and then he laughed. He is still a young man, of course." Timofey Semyonitch blew his nose with a loud noise. "And yet, young though he is, what a career he is making for himself."

"That's quite a different thing, Timofey Semyonitch."

"Of course, of course."

"Well, what do you say then, Timofey Semyonitch?"

"Why, what can I do?"

"Give advice, guidance, as a man of experience, a relative! What are we to do? What steps are we to take? Go to the authorities and..."

"To the authorities? Certainly not," Timofey Semyonitch replied hurriedly. "If you ask my advice, you had better, above all, hush the matter up and act, so to speak, as a private person. It is a suspicious incident, quite unheard of. Unheard of, above all; there is no precedent for it, and it is far from creditable.... And so discretion above all.... Let him lie there a bit. We must wait and see...."

"But how can we wait and see, Timofey Semyonitch? What if he is stifled there?"

"Why should he be? I think you told me that he made himself fairly comfortable there?"

I told him the whole story over again. Timofey Semyonitch pondered.

"Hm!" he said, twisting his snuffbox in his hands. "To my mind it's really a good thing he should lie there a bit, instead of going abroad. Let him reflect at his leisure. Of course he mustn't be stifled, and so he must take measures to preserve his health, avoiding a cough, for instance, and so on.... And as for the German, it's my personal opinion he is within his rights, and even more so than the other side, because it was the other party who got into *his* crocodile without asking permission, and not *he* who got into Ivan Matveitch's crocodile without asking permission, though, so far as I recollect, the latter has no crocodile. And a crocodile is private property, and so it is impossible to slit him open without compensation."

"For the saving of human life, Timofey Semyonitch."

"Oh, well, that's a matter for the police. You must go to them."

"But Ivan Matveitch may be needed in the department. He may be asked for."

"Ivan Matveitch needed? Ha-ha! Besides, he is on leave, so that we may ignore him — let him inspect the countries of Europe! It will be a different matter if he doesn't turn up when his leave is over. Then we shall ask for him and make inquiries."

"Three months! Timofey Semyonitch, for pity's sake!"

"It's his own fault. Nobody thrust him there. At this rate we should have to get a nurse to look after him at government expense, and that is not allowed for in the regulations. But the chief point is that the crocodile is private property, so that the principles of economics apply in this question. And the principles of economics are paramount. Only the other evening, at Luka Andreitch's, Ignaty Prokofyitch was saying so. Do you know Ignaty Prokofyitch? A capitalist, in a big way of business, and he speaks so fluently. 'We need industrial development,' he said; 'there is very little development among us. We must create it. We must create capital, so we must create a middle-class, the so-called bourgeoisie. And as we haven't capital we must attract it from abroad. We must, in the first place, give facilities to foreign companies to buy up lands in Russia as is done now abroad. The communal holding of land is poison, is ruin.' And, you know, he spoke with such heat; well, that's all right for him — a wealthy man, and not in the service. 'With the communal system,' he said, 'there will be no improvement in industrial development or agriculture. Foreign companies,' he said, 'must as far as possible buy up the whole of our land in big lots, and then split it up, split it up, split it up, in the smallest parts possible' — and do you know he pronounced the words 'split it up' with such determination —'and then sell it as private property. Or rather, not sell it, but simply let it. When,' he said, 'all the land is in the hands of foreign companies they can fix any rent they like. And so the peasant will work three times as much for his daily bread and he can be turned out at pleasure. So that he will feel it, will be submissive and industrious, and will work three times as much for the same wages. But as it is, with the commune, what does he care? He knows he won't die of hunger, so he is lazy and drunken. And meanwhile money will be attracted into Russia, capital will be created and the bourgeoisie will spring up. The English political and literary paper, *The Times*, in an article the other day on our finances stated that the reason our financial position was so unsatisfactory was that we had no middle-class, no big fortunes, no accommodating proletariat.' Ignaty Prokofyitch speaks well. He is an orator. He wants to lay a report on the subject before the authorities, and then to get it published in the *News*. That's something very different from verses like Ivan Matveitch's...."

"But how about Ivan Matveitch?" I put in, after letting the old man babble on.

Timofey Semyonitch was sometimes fond of talking and showing that he was not behind the times, but knew all about things.

"How about Ivan Matveitch? Why, I am coming to that. Here we are, anxious to bring foreign capital into the country — and only consider: as soon as the capital of a foreigner, who has been attracted to Petersburg, has been doubled through Ivan Matveitch, instead of protecting the foreign capitalist, we are proposing to rip open the belly of his original capital — the crocodile. Is it consistent? To my mind, Ivan Matveitch, as the true son of his fatherland, ought to rejoice and to be proud that through him the value of a foreign crocodile has been doubled and possibly even trebled. That's just what is wanted to attract capital. If one man succeeds, mind you, another will come with a crocodile, and a third will bring two or three of them at once, and capital will grow up about them — there you have a bourgeoisie. It must be encouraged."

"Upon my word, Timofey Semyonitch!" I cried, "you are demanding almost supernatural self-sacrifice from poor Ivan Matveitch."

"I demand nothing, and I beg you, before everything — as I have said already — to remember that I am not a person in authority and so cannot demand anything of any one. I am speaking as a son of the fatherland, that is, not as the *Son of the Fatherland*, but as a son of the fatherland. Again, what possessed him to get into the crocodile? A respectable man, a man of good grade in the service, lawfully married — and then to behave like that! Is it consistent?"

"But it was an accident."

"Who knows? And where is the money to compensate the owner to come from?"

"Perhaps out of his salary, Timofey Semyonitch?"

"Would that be enough?"

"No, it wouldn't, Timofey Semyonitch," I answered sadly. "The proprietor was at first alarmed that the crocodile would burst, but as soon as he was sure that it was all right, he began to bluster and was delighted to think that he could double the charge for entry."

"Treble and quadruple perhaps! The public will simply stampede the place now, and crocodile owners are smart people. Besides, it's not Lent yet, and people are keen on diversions, and so I say again, the great thing is that Ivan Matveitch should preserve his incognito, don't let him be in a hurry. Let everybody know, perhaps, that he is in the crocodile, but don't let them be officially informed of it. Ivan Matveitch is in particularly favourable circumstances for that, for he is reckoned to be abroad. It will be said he is in the crocodile, and we will refuse to believe it. That is how it can be managed. The great thing is that he should wait; and why should he be in a hurry?"

"Well, but if..."

"Don't worry, he has a good constitution...."

"Well, and afterwards, when he has waited?"

"Well, I won't conceal from you that the case is exceptional in the highest degree. One doesn't know what to think of it, and the worst of it is there is no precedent. If we had a precedent we might have something to go by. But as it is, what is one to say? It will certainly take time to settle it."

A happy thought flashed upon my mind.

"Cannot we arrange," I said, "that if he is destined to remain in the entrails of the monster and it is the will of Providence that he should remain alive, that he should send in a petition to be reckoned as still serving?"

"Hm!...Possibly as on leave and without salary...."

"But couldn't it be with salary?"

"On what grounds?"

"As sent on a special commission."

"What commission and where?"

"Why, into the entrails, the entrails of the crocodile.... So to speak, for exploration, for investigation of the facts on the spot. It would, of course, be a novelty, but that is progressive and would at the same time show zeal for enlightenment."

Timofey Semyonitch thought a little.

"To send a special official," he said at last, "to the inside of a crocodile to conduct a special inquiry is, in my personal opinion, an absurdity. It is not in the regulations. And what sort of special inquiry could there be there?"

"The scientific study of nature on the spot, in the living subject. The natural sciences are all the fashion nowadays, botany.... He could live there and report his observations.... For instance, concerning digestion or simply habits. For the sake of accumulating facts."

"You mean as statistics. Well, I am no great authority on that subject, indeed I am no philosopher at all. You say 'facts' — we are overwhelmed with facts as it is, and don't know what to do with them. Besides, statistics are a danger."

"In what way?"

"They are a danger. Moreover, you will admit he will report facts, so to speak, lying like a log. And, can one do one's official duties lying like a log? That would be another novelty and a dangerous one; and again, there is no precedent for it. If we had any sort of precedent for it, then, to my thinking, he might have been given the job."

"But no live crocodiles have been brought over hitherto, Timofey Semyonitch."

"Hm...yes," he reflected again. "Your objection is a just one, if you like, and might indeed serve as a ground for carrying the matter further; but consider again, that if with the arrival of living crocodiles government clerks begin to disappear, and then on the ground that they are warm and comfortable there, expect to receive the official sanction for their position, and then take their ease there...you must admit it would be a bad example. We should have every one trying to go the same way to get a salary for nothing."

"Do your best for him, Timofey Semyonitch. By the way, Ivan Matveitch asked me to give you seven roubles he had lost to you at cards."

"Ah, he lost that the other day at Nikifor Nikiforitch's. I remember. And how gay and amusing he was — and now!"

The old man was genuinely touched.

"Intercede for him, Timofey Semyonitch!"

"I will do my best. I will speak in my own name, as a private person, as though I were asking for information. And meanwhile, you find out indirectly, unofficially, how much would the proprietor consent to take for his crocodile?"

Timofey Semyonitch was visibly more friendly.

"Certainly," I answered. "And I will come back to you at once to report."

"And his wife...is she alone now? Is she depressed?"

"You should call on her, Timofey Semyonitch."

"I will. I thought of doing so before; it's a good opportunity.... And what on earth possessed him to go and look at the crocodile? Though, indeed, I should like to see it myself."

"Go and see the poor fellow, Timofey Semyonitch."

"I will. Of course, I don't want to raise his hopes by doing so. I shall go as a private person.... Well, goodbye, I am going to Nikifor Nikiforitch's again: shall you be there?"

"No, I am going to see the poor prisoner."

"Yes, now he is a prisoner!...Ah, that's what comes of thoughtlessness!"

I said goodbye to the old man. Ideas of all kinds were straying through my mind. A good-natured and most honest man, Timofey Semyonitch, yet, as I left him, I felt pleased at the thought that he had celebrated his fiftieth year of service, and that Timofey Semyonitchs are now a rarity among us. I flew at once, of course, to the Arcade to tell poor Ivan Matveitch all the news. And, indeed, I was moved by curiosity to know how he was getting on in the crocodile and how it was possible to live in a crocodile. And, indeed, was it possible to live in a crocodile at all? At times it really seemed to me as though it were all an outlandish, monstrous dream, especially as an outlandish monster was the chief figure in it.

III

And yet it was not a dream, but actual, indubitable fact. Should I be telling the story if it were not? But to continue.

It was late, about nine o'clock, before I reached the Arcade, and I had to go into the crocodile room by the back entrance, for the German had closed the shop earlier than usual that evening. Now in the seclusion of domesticity he was walking about in a greasy old frockcoat, but he seemed three times as pleased as he had been in the morning. It was evidently that he had no apprehensions now, and that the public had been coming "many more." The *Mutter* came out later, evidently to keep an eye on me. The German and the *Mutter* frequently whispered together. Although the shop was closed he charged me a quarter-rouble! What unnecessary exactitude!

"You will every time pay; the public will one rouble, and you one quarter pay; for you are the good friend of your good friend; and I a friend respect...."

"Are you alive, are you alive, my cultured friend?" I cried, as I approached the crocodile, expecting my words to reach Ivan Matveitch from a distance and to flatter his vanity.

"Alive and well," he answered, as though from a long way off or from under the bed, though I was standing close beside him. "Alive and well; but of that later.... How are things going?"

As though purposely not hearing the question, I was just beginning with sympathetic haste to question him how he was, what it was like in the crocodile, and what, in fact, there was inside a crocodile. Both friendship and common civility demanded this. But with capricious annoyance he interrupted me.

"How are things going?" he shouted, in a shrill and on this occasion particularly revolting voice, addressing me peremptorily as usual.

I described to him my whole conversation with Timofey Semyonitch down to the smallest detail. As I told my story I tried to show my resentment in my voice.

"The old man is right," Ivan Matveitch pronounced as abruptly as usual in his conversation with me. "I like practical people, and can't endure sentimental milksops. I am ready to admit, however, that your idea about a special commission is not altogether absurd. I certainly have a great deal to report, both from a scientific and from an ethical point of view. But now all this has taken a new and unexpected aspect, and it is not worth while to trouble about mere salary. Listen attentively. Are you sitting down?"

"No, I am standing up."

"Sit down on the floor if there is nothing else, and listen attentively."

Resentfully I took a chair and put it down on the floor with a bang, in my anger.

"Listen," he began dictatorially. "The public came to-day in masses. There was no room left in the evening, and the police came in to keep order. At eight o'clock, that is, earlier than usual, the proprietor thought it necessary to close the shop and end the exhibition to count the money he had taken and prepare for tomorrow more conveniently. So I know there will be a regular fair tomorrow. So we may assume that all the most cultivated people in the capital, the ladies of the best society, the foreign ambassadors, the leading lawyers and so on, will all be present. What's more, people will be flowing here from the remotest provinces of our vast and interesting empire. The upshot of it is that I am the cynosure of all eyes, and though hidden to sight, I am eminent. I shall teach the idle crowd. Taught by experience, I shall be an example of greatness and resignation to fate! I shall be, so to say, a pulpit from which to instruct mankind. The mere biological details I can furnish about the monster I am inhabiting are of priceless value. And so, far from repining at what has happened, I confidently hope for the most brilliant of careers."

"You won't find it wearisome?" I asked sarcastically.

What irritated me more than anything was the extreme pomposity of his language. Nevertheless, it all rather disconcerted me. "What on earth, what, can this frivolous blockhead find to be so cocky about?" I muttered to myself. "He ought to be crying instead of being cocky."

"No!" he answered my observation sharply, "for I am full of great ideas, only now can I at leisure ponder over the amelioration of the lot of humanity. Truth and light will come forth now from the crocodile. I shall certainly develop a new economic theory of my own and I shall be proud of it — which I have hitherto been prevented from doing by my official duties and by trivial distractions. I shall refute everything and be a new Fourier. By the way, did you give Timofey Semyonitch the seven roubles?"

"Yes, out of my own pocket," I answered, trying to emphasise that fact in my voice.

"We will settle it," he answered superciliously. "I confidently expect my salary to be raised, for who should get a raise if not I? I am of the utmost service now. But to business. My wife?"

"You are, I suppose, inquiring after Elena Ivanovna?"

"My wife?" he shouted, this time in a positive squeal.

There was no help for it! Meekly, though gnashing my teeth, I told him how I had left Elena Ivanovna. He did not even hear me out.

"I have special plans in regard to her," he began impatiently. "If I am celebrated *here*, I wish her to be celebrated *there*. Savants, poets, philosophers, foreign mineralogists, statesmen, after conversing in the morning with me, will visit her *salon* in the evening. From next week onwards she must have an 'At Home' every evening. With my salary doubled, we shall have the means for entertaining, and as the entertainment must not go beyond tea and hired footmen — that's settled. Both here and there they will talk of me. I have long thirsted for an opportunity for being talked about, but could not attain it, fettered by my humble position and low grade in the service. And now all this has been attained by a simple gulp on the part of the crocodile. Every word of mine will be listened to, every utterance will be thought over, repeated, printed. And I'll teach them what I am worth! They shall understand at last what abilities they have allowed to vanish in the entrails of a monster. 'This man might have been Foreign Minister or might have ruled a kingdom,' some will say. 'And that man did not rule a kingdom,' others will say. In what way am I inferior to a Garnier-Pagesishky or whatever they are called? My wife must be a worthy second — I have brains, she has beauty and charm. 'She is beautiful, and that is why she is his wife,' some will say. 'She is beautiful *because* she is his wife,' others will amend. To be ready for anything let Elena Ivanovna buy tomorrow the Encyclopædia edited by Andrey Kraevsky, that she may be able to converse on any topic. Above all, let her be sure to read the political leader in the *Petersburg News*, comparing it every day with the *Voice*. I imagine that the proprietor will consent to take me sometimes with the crocodile to my wife's brilliant *salon*. I will be in a tank in the middle of the magnificent drawing-room, and I will scintillate with witticisms which I will prepare in the morning. To the statesmen I will impart my projects; to the poet I will speak in rhyme; with the ladies I can be amusing and charming without impropriety, since I shall be no danger to their husbands' peace of mind. To all the rest I shall serve as a pattern of resignation to fate and the will of Providence. I shall make my wife a brilliant literary lady; I shall bring her forward and explain her to the public; as my wife she must be full of the most striking virtues; and if they are right in calling Andrey Alexandrovitch our Russian Alfred de Musset, they will be still more right in calling her our Russian Yevgenia Tour."

I must confess that although this wild nonsense was rather in Ivan Matveitch's habitual style, it did occur to me that he was in a fever and delirious. It was the same, everyday Ivan Matveitch, but magnified twenty times.

"My friend," I asked him, "are you hoping for a long life? Tell me, in fact, are you well? How do you eat, how do you sleep, how do you breathe? I am your friend, and you must admit that the incident is most unnatural, and consequently my curiosity is most natural."

"Idle curiosity and nothing else," he pronounced sententiously, "but you shall be satisfied. You ask how I am managing in the entrails of the monster? To begin with, the crocodile, to my amusement, turns out to be perfectly empty. His inside consists of a sort of huge empty sack made of gutta-percha, like the elastic goods sold in the Gorohovy Street, in the Morskaya, and, if I am not mistaken, in the Voznesensky Prospect. Otherwise, if you think of it, how could I find room?"

"Is it possible?" I cried, in a surprise that may well be understood. "Can the crocodile be perfectly empty?"

"Perfectly," Ivan Matveitch maintained sternly and impressively. "And in all probability, it is so constructed by the laws of Nature. The crocodile possesses nothing but jaws furnished with sharp teeth, and besides the jaws, a tail of considerable length — that is all, properly speaking. The middle part between these two extremities is an empty space enclosed by something of the nature of gutta-percha, probably really gutta-percha."

"But the ribs, the stomach, the intestines, the liver, the heart?" I interrupted quite angrily.

"There is nothing, absolutely nothing of all that, and probably there never has been. All that is the idle fancy of frivolous travellers. As one inflates an air-cushion, I am now with my person inflating the crocodile. He is incredibly elastic. Indeed, you might, as the friend of the family, get in with me if you were generous and self-sacrificing enough — and even with you here there would be room to spare. I even think that in the last resort I might send for Elena Ivanovna. However, this void, hollow formation of the crocodile is quite in keeping with the teachings of natural science. If, for instance, one had to construct a new crocodile, the question would naturally present itself. What is the fundamental characteristic of the crocodile? The answer is clear: to swallow human beings. How is one, in constructing the crocodile, to secure that he should swallow people? The answer is clearer still: construct him hollow. It was settled by physics long ago that Nature abhors a vacuum. Hence the inside of the crocodile must be hollow so that it may abhor the vacuum, and consequently swallow and so fill itself with anything it can come across. And that is the sole rational cause why every crocodile swallows men. It is not the same in the constitution of man: the emptier a man's head is, for instance, the less he feels the thirst to fill it, and that is the one exception to the general rule. It is all as clear as day to me now. I have deduced it by my own observation and experience, being, so to say, in the very bowels of Nature, in its retort, listening to the throbbing of its pulse. Even etymology supports me, for the very word crocodile means voracity. Crocodile — *crocodillo* — is evidently an Italian word, dating perhaps from the Egyptian Pharaohs, and evidently derived from the French verb *croquer*, which means to eat, to devour, in general to absorb nourishment. All these remarks I intend to deliver as my first lecture in Elena Ivanovna's *salon* when they take me there in the tank."

"My friend, oughtn't you at least to take some purgative?" I cried involuntarily.

"He is in a fever, a fever, he is feverish!" I repeated to myself in alarm.

"Nonsense!" he answered contemptuously. "Besides, in my present position it would be most inconvenient. I knew, though, you would be sure to talk of taking medicine."

"But, my friend, how…how do you take food now? Have you dined to-day?"

"No, but I am not hungry, and most likely I shall never take food again. And that, too, is quite natural; filling the whole interior of the crocodile I make him feel always full. Now he need not be fed for some years. On the other hand, nourished by me, he will naturally impart to me all the vital juices of his body; it is the same as with some accomplished coquettes who embed themselves and their whole persons for the night in raw steak, and then, after their morning bath, are fresh, supple, buxom and fascinating. In that way nourishing the crocodile, I myself obtain nourishment from him, consequently we mutually nourish one another. But as it is difficult even for a crocodile to digest a man like me, he must, no doubt, be conscious of a certain weight in his stomach — an organ which he does not, however, possess — and that is why, to avoid causing the creature suffering, I do not often turn over, and although I could turn over I do not do so from humanitarian motives. This is the one drawback of my present position, and in an allegorical sense Timofey Semyonitch was right in saying I was lying like a log. But I will prove that even lying like a log — nay, that only lying like a log — one can revolutionise the lot of mankind. All the great ideas and movements of our newspapers and magazines have evidently been the work of men who were lying like logs; that is why they call them divorced from the realities of life — but what does it matter, their saying that! I am constructing now a complete system of my own, and you wouldn't believe how easy it is! You have only to creep into a secluded corner or into a crocodile, to shut your eyes, and you immediately devise a perfect millennium for mankind. When you went away this afternoon I set to work at once and have already invented three systems, now I am preparing the fourth. It is true that at first one must refute everything that has gone before, but from the crocodile it is so easy to refute it; besides, it all becomes clearer, seen from the inside of the crocodile.... There are some drawbacks, though small ones, in my position, however; it is somewhat damp here and covered with a sort of slime; moreover, there is a smell of india-rubber like the smell of my old galoshes. That is all, there are no other drawbacks."

"Ivan Matveitch," I interrupted, "all this is a miracle in which I can scarcely believe. And can you, can you intend never to dine again?"

"What trivial nonsense you are troubling about, you thoughtless, frivolous creature! I talk to you about great ideas, and you.... Understand that I am sufficiently nourished by the great ideas which light up the darkness in which I am enveloped. The goodnatured proprietor has, however, after consulting the kindly *Mutter*, decided with her that they will every morning insert into the monster's jaws a bent metal tube, something like a whistle pipe, by means of which I can absorb coffee or broth with bread soaked in it. The pipe has already been bespoken in the neighbourhood, but I think this is superfluous luxury. I hope to live at least a thousand years, if it is true that crocodiles live so long, which, by the way — good thing I thought of it — you had better look up in some natural history tomorrow and tell me, for I may have been mistaken and have mixed it up with some excavated monster. There is only one reflection rather troubles me: as I am dressed in cloth and have boots on, the crocodile can obviously not digest me. Besides, I am alive, and so am opposing the process of digestion with my whole will power; for you can understand that I do not wish to be turned into what all nourishment turns into, for that would be too humiliating for me. But there is one thing I am afraid of: in a thousand years the cloth of my coat, unfortunately of Russian make, may decay, and then, left without clothing, I might perhaps, in spite of my indignation, begin to be digested; and though by day nothing would induce me to allow it, at night, in my sleep, when a man's will deserts him, I may be overtaken by the humiliating destiny of a potato, a pancake, or veal. Such an idea reduces me to fury. This alone is an argument for the revision of the tariff and the encouragement of the importation of English cloth, which is stronger and so will withstand Nature longer when one is swallowed by a crocodile. At the first opportunity I will impart this idea to some statesman and at the same time to the political writers on our Petersburg dailies. Let them publish it abroad. I trust this will not be the only idea they will borrow from me. I foresee that every morning a regular crowd of them, provided with quarter-roubles from the editorial office, will be flocking round me to seize my ideas on the telegrams of the previous day. In brief, the future presents itself to me in the rosiest light."

"Fever, fever!" I whispered to myself.

"My friend, and freedom?" I asked, wishing to learn his views thoroughly. "You are, so to speak, in prison, while every man has a right to the enjoyment of freedom."

"You are a fool," he answered. "Savages love independence, wise men love order; and if there is no order...."

"Ivan Matveitch, spare me, please!"

"Hold your tongue and listen!" he squealed, vexed at my interrupting him. "Never has my spirit soared as now. In my narrow refuge there is only one thing that I dread — the literary criticisms of the monthlies and the hiss of our satirical papers. I am afraid that thoughtless visitors, stupid and envious people and nihilists in general, may turn me into ridicule. But I will take measures. I am impatiently awaiting the response of the public tomorrow, and especially the opinion of the newspapers. You must tell me about the papers tomorrow."

"Very good; tomorrow I will bring a perfect pile of papers with me."

"Tomorrow it is too soon to expect reports in the newspapers, for it will take four days for it to be advertised. But from to-day come to me every evening by the back way through the yard. I am intending to employ you as my secretary. You shall read the newspapers and magazines to me, and I will dictate to you my ideas and give you commissions. Be particularly careful not to forget the foreign telegrams. Let all the European telegrams be here every day. But enough; most likely you are sleepy by now. Go home, and do not think of what I said just now about criticisms: I am not afraid of it, for the critics themselves are in a critical position. One has only to be wise and virtuous and one will certainly get on to a pedestal. If not Socrates, then Diogenes, or perhaps both of them together — that is my future rôle among mankind."

So frivolously and boastfully did Ivan Matveitch hasten to express himself before me, like feverish weak-willed women who, as we are told by the proverb, cannot keep a secret. All that he told me about the crocodile struck me as most suspicious. How was it possible that the crocodile was absolutely hollow? I don't mind betting that he was bragging from vanity and partly to humiliate me. It is true that he was an invalid and one must make allowances for invalids; but I must frankly confess, I never could endure Ivan Matveitch. I have been trying all my life, from a child up, to escape from his tutelage and have not been able to! A thousand times over I have been tempted to break with him altogether, and every time I have been drawn to him again, as though I were still hoping to prove something to him or to revenge myself on him. A strange thing, this friendship! I can positively assert that nine-tenths of my friendship for him was made up of malice. On this occasion, however, we parted with genuine feeling.

"Your friend a very clever man!" the German said to me in an undertone as he moved to see me out; he had been listening all the time attentively to our conversation.

"*À propos*," I said, "while I think of it: how much would you ask for your crocodile in case any one wanted to buy it?"

Ivan Matveitch, who heard the question, was waiting with curiosity for the answer; it was evident that he did not want the German to ask too little; anyway, he cleared his throat in a peculiar way on hearing my question.

At first the German would not listen — was positively angry.

"No one will dare my own crocodile to buy!" he cried furiously, and turned as red as a boiled lobster. "Me not want to sell the crocodile! I would not for the crocodile a million thalers take. I took a hundred and thirty thalers from the public to-day, and I shall tomorrow ten thousand take, and then a hundred thousand every day I shall take. I will not him sell."

Ivan Matveitch positively chuckled with satisfaction. Controlling myself — for I felt it was a duty to my friend — I hinted coolly and reasonably to the crazy German that his calculations were not quite correct, that if he makes a hundred thousand every day, all Petersburg will have visited him in four days, and then there will be no one left to bring him roubles, that life and death are in God's hands, that the crocodile may burst or Ivan Matveitch may fall ill and die, and so on and so on.

The German grew pensive.

"I will him drops from the chemist's get," he said, after pondering, "and will save your friend that he die not."

"Drops are all very well," I answered, "but consider, too, that the thing may get into the law courts. Ivan Matveitch's wife may demand the restitution of her lawful spouse. You are intending to get rich, but do you intend to give Elena Ivanovna a pension?"

"No, me not intend," said the German in stern decision.

"No, we not intend," said the *Mutter*, with positive malignancy.

"And so would it not be better for you to accept something now, at once, a secure and solid though moderate sum, than to leave things to chance? I ought to tell you that I am inquiring simply from curiosity."

The German drew the *Mutter* aside to consult with her in a corner where there stood a case with the largest and ugliest monkey of his collection.

"Well, you will see!" said Ivan Matveitch.

As for me, I was at that moment burning with the desire, first, to give the German a thrashing, next, to give the *Mutter* an even sounder one, and, thirdly, to give Ivan Matveitch the soundest thrashing of all for his boundless vanity. But all this paled beside the answer of the rapacious German.

After consultation with the *Mutter* he demanded for his crocodile fifty thousand roubles in bonds of the last Russian loan with lottery voucher attached, a brick house in Gorohovy Street with a chemist's shop attached, and in addition the rank of Russian colonel.

"You see!" Ivan Matveitch cried triumphantly. "I told you so! Apart from this last senseless desire for the rank of a colonel, he is perfectly right, for he fully understands the present value of the monster he is exhibiting. The economic principle before everything!"

"Upon my word!" I cried furiously to the German. "But what should you be made a colonel for? What exploit have you performed? What service have you done? In what way have you gained military glory? You are really crazy!"

"Crazy!" cried the German, offended. "No, a person very sensible, but you very stupid! I have a colonel deserved for that I have a crocodile shown and in him a live *hofrath* sitting! And a Russian can a crocodile not show and a live *hofrath* in him sitting! Me extremely clever man and much wish colonel to be!"

"Well, goodbye, then, Ivan Matveitch!" I cried, shaking with fury, and I went out of the crocodile room almost at a run.

I felt that in another minute I could not have answered for myself. The unnatural expectations of these two blockheads were insupportable. The cold air refreshed me and somewhat moderated my indignation. At last, after spitting vigorously fifteen times on each side, I took a cab, got home, undressed and flung myself into bed. What vexed me more than anything was my having become his secretary. Now I was to die of boredom there every evening, doing the duty of a true friend! I was ready to beat myself for it, and I did, in fact, after putting out the candle and pulling up the bedclothes, punch myself several times on the head and various parts of my body. That somewhat relieved me, and at last I fell asleep fairly soundly, in fact, for I was very tired. All night long I could dream of nothing but monkeys, but towards morning I dreamt of Elena Ivanovna.

IV

The monkeys I dreamed about, I surmise, because they were shut up in the case at the German's; but Elena Ivanovna was a different story.

I may as well say at once, I loved the lady, but I make haste — post-haste — to make a qualification. I loved her as a father, neither more nor less. I judge that because I often felt an irresistible desire to kiss her little head or her rosy cheek. And though I never carried out this inclination, I would not have refused even to kiss her lips. And not merely her lips, but her teeth, which always gleamed so charmingly like two rows of pretty, well-matched pearls when she laughed. She laughed extraordinarily often. Ivan Matveitch in demonstrative moments used to call her his "darling absurdity" — a name extremely happy and appropriate. She was a perfect sugarplum, and that was all one could say of her. Therefore I am utterly at a loss to understand what possessed Ivan Matveitch to imagine his wife as a Russian Yevgenia Tour? Anyway, my dream, with the exception of the monkeys, left a most pleasant impression upon me, and going over all the incidents of the previous day as I drank my morning cup of tea, I resolved to go and see Elena Ivanovna at once on my way to the office — which, indeed, I was bound to do as the friend of the family.

In a tiny little room out of the bedroom — the so-called little drawing-room, though their big drawing-room was little too — Elena Ivanovna was sitting, in some half-transparent morning wrapper, on a smart little sofa before a little tea-table, drinking coffee out of a little cup in which she was dipping a minute biscuit. She was ravishingly pretty, but struck me as being at the same time rather pensive.

"Ah, that's you, naughty man!" she said, greeting me with an absentminded smile. "Sit down, featherhead, have some coffee. Well, what were you doing yesterday? Were you at the masquerade?"

"Why, were you? I don't go, you know. Besides, yesterday I was visiting our captive...." I sighed and assumed a pious expression as I took the coffee.

"Whom?...What captive?...Oh, yes! Poor fellow! Well, how is he — bored? Do you know... I wanted to ask you.... I suppose I can ask for a divorce now?"

"A divorce!" I cried in indignation and almost spilled the coffee. "It's that swarthy fellow," I thought to myself bitterly.

There was a certain swarthy gentleman with little moustaches who was something in the architectural line, and who came far too often to see them, and was extremely skilful in amusing Elena Ivanovna. I must confess I hated him and there was no doubt that he had succeeded in seeing Elena Ivanovna yesterday either at the masquerade or even here, and putting all sorts of nonsense into her head.

"Why," Elena Ivanovna rattled off hurriedly, as though it were a lesson she had learnt, "if he is going to stay on in the crocodile, perhaps not come back all his life, while I sit waiting for him here! A husband ought to live at home, and not in a crocodile...."

"But this was an unforeseen occurrence," I was beginning, in very comprehensible agitation.

"Oh, no, don't talk to me, I won't listen, I won't listen," she cried, suddenly getting quite cross. "You are always against me, you wretch! There's no doing anything with you, you will never give me any advice! Other people tell me that I can get a divorce because Ivan Matveitch will not get his salary now."

"Elena Ivanovna! is it you I hear!" I exclaimed pathetically. "What villain could have put such an idea into your head? And divorce on such a trivial ground as a salary is quite impossible. And poor Ivan Matveitch, poor Ivan Matveitch is, so to speak, burning with love for you even in the bowels of the monster. What's more, he is melting away with love like a lump of sugar. Yesterday while you were enjoying yourself at the masquerade, he was saying that he might in the last resort send for you as his lawful spouse to join him in the entrails of the monster, especially as it appears the crocodile is exceedingly roomy, not only able to accommodate two but even three persons...."

And then I told her all that interesting part of my conversation the night before with Ivan Matveitch.

"What, what!" she cried, in surprise. "You want me to get into the monster too, to be with Ivan Matveitch? What an idea! And how am I to get in there, in my hat and crinoline? Heavens, what foolishness! And what should I look like while I was getting into it, and very likely there would be some one there to see me! It's absurd! And what should I have to eat there? And... and...and what should I do there when.... Oh, my goodness, what will they think of next?... And what should I have to amuse me there?...You say there's a smell of gutta-percha? And what should I do if we quarrelled — should we have to go on staying there side by side? Foo, how horrid!"

"I agree, I agree with all those arguments, my sweet Elena Ivanovna," I interrupted, striving to express myself with that natural enthusiasm which always overtakes a man when he feels the truth is on his side. "But one thing you have not appreciated in all this, you have not realised that he cannot live without you if he is inviting you there; that is a proof of love, passionate, faithful, ardent love.... You have thought too little of his love, dear Elena Ivanovna!"

"I won't, I won't, I won't hear anything about it!" waving me off with her pretty little hand with glistening pink nails that had just been washed and polished. "Horrid man! You will reduce me to tears! Get into it yourself, if you like the prospect. You are his friend, get in and keep him company, and spend your life discussing some tedious science...."

"You are wrong to laugh at this suggestion" — I checked the frivolous woman with dignity — "Ivan Matveitch has invited me as it is. You, of course, are summoned there by duty; for me, it would be an act of generosity. But when Ivan Matveitch described to me last night the elasticity of the crocodile, he hinted very plainly that there would be room not only for you two, but for me also as a friend of the family, especially if I wished to join you, and therefore...."

"How so, the three of us?" cried Elena Ivanovna, looking at me in surprise. "Why, how should we...are we going to be all three there together? Ha-ha-ha! How silly you both are! Ha-ha-ha! I shall certainly pinch you all the time, you wretch! Ha-ha-ha! Ha-ha-ha!"

And falling back on the sofa, she laughed till she cried. All this — the tears and the laughter — were so fascinating that I could not resist rushing eagerly to kiss her hand, which she did not oppose, though she did pinch my ears lightly as a sign of reconciliation.

Then we both grew very cheerful, and I described to her in detail all Ivan Matveitch's plans. The thought of her evening receptions and her *salon* pleased her very much.

"Only I should need a great many new dresses," she observed, "and so Ivan Matveitch must send me as much of his salary as possible and as soon as possible. Only...only I don't know about that," she added thoughtfully. "How can he be brought here in the tank? That's very absurd. I don't want my husband to be carried about in a tank. I should feel quite ashamed for my visitors to see it.... I don't want that, no, I don't."

"By the way, while I think of it, was Timofey Semyonitch here yesterday?"

"Oh, yes, he was; he came to comfort me, and do you know, we played cards all the time. He played for sweetmeats, and if I lost he was to kiss my hands. What a wretch he is! And only fancy, he almost came to the masquerade with me, really!"

"He was carried away by his feelings!" I observed. "And who would not be with you, you charmer?"

"Oh, get along with your compliments! Stay, I'll give you a pinch as a parting present. I've learnt to pinch awfully well lately. Well, what do you say to that? By the way, you say Ivan Matveitch spoke several times of me yesterday?"

"N-no, not exactly.... I must say he is thinking more now of the fate of humanity, and wants...."

"Oh, let him! You needn't go on! I am sure it's fearfully boring. I'll go and see him some time. I shall certainly go tomorrow. Only not to-day; I've got a headache, and besides, there will be such a lot of people there to-day.... They'll say, 'That's his wife,' and I shall feel ashamed.... Goodbye. You will be...there this evening, won't you?"

"To see him, yes. He asked me to go and take him the papers."

"That's capital. Go and read to him. But don't come and see me to-day. I am not well, and perhaps I may go and see some one. Goodbye, you naughty man."

"It's that swarthy fellow is going to see her this evening," I thought.

At the office, of course, I gave no sign of being consumed by these cares and anxieties. But soon I noticed some of the most progressive papers seemed to be passing particularly rapidly from hand to hand among my colleagues, and were being read with an extremely serious expression of face. The first one that reached me was the *News-sheet*, a paper of no particular party but humanitarian in general, for which it was regarded with contempt among us, though it was read. Not without surprise I read in it the following paragraph:

"Yesterday strange rumours were circulating among the spacious ways and sumptuous buildings of our vast metropolis. A certain well-known *bon-vivant* of the highest society, probably weary of the *cuisine* at Borel's and at the X. Club, went into the Arcade, into the place where an immense crocodile recently brought to the metropolis is being exhibited, and insisted on its being prepared for his dinner. After bargaining with the proprietor he at once set to work to devour him (that is, not the proprietor, a very meek and punctilious German, but his crocodile), cutting juicy morsels with his penknife from the living animal, and swallowing them with extraordinary rapidity. By degrees the whole crocodile disappeared into the vast recesses of his stomach, so that he was even on the point of attacking an ichneumon, a constant companion of the crocodile, probably imagining that the latter would be as savoury. We are by no means opposed to that new article of diet with which foreign *gourmands* have long been familiar. We have, indeed, predicted that it would come. English lords and travellers make up regular parties for catching crocodiles in Egypt, and consume the back of the monster cooked like beefsteak, with mustard, onions and potatoes. The French who followed in the train of Lesseps prefer the paws baked-in hot ashes, which they do, however, in opposition to the English, who laugh at them. Probably both ways would be appreciated among us. For our part, we are delighted at a new branch of industry, of which our great and varied fatherland stands preeminently in need. Probably before a year is out crocodiles will be brought in hundreds to replace this first one, lost in the stomach of a Petersburg *gourmand*. And why should not the crocodile be acclimatised among us in Russia? If the water of the Neva is too cold for these interesting strangers, there are ponds in the capital and rivers and lakes outside it. Why not breed crocodiles at Pargolovo, for instance, or at Pavlovsk, in the Presnensky Ponds and in Samoteka in Moscow? While providing agreeable, wholesome nourishment for our fastidious *gourmands*, they might at the same time entertain the ladies who walk about these ponds and instruct the children in natural history. The crocodile skin might be used for making jewel-cases, boxes, cigar-cases, pocket-books, and possibly more than one thousand saved up in the greasy notes that are peculiarly beloved of merchants might be laid by in crocodile skin. We hope to return more than once to this interesting topic."

Though I had foreseen something of the sort, yet the reckless inaccuracy of the paragraph overwhelmed me. Finding no one with whom to share my impression, I turned to Prohor Savvitch who was sitting opposite to me, and noticed that the latter had been watching me for some time, while in his hand he held the *Voice* as though he were on the point of passing it to me. Without a word he took the *News-sheet* from me, and as he handed me the *Voice* he drew a line with his nail against an article to which he probably wished to call my attention. This Prohor Savvitch was a very queer man: a taciturn old bachelor, he was not on intimate terms with any of us, scarcely spoke to any one in the office, always had an opinion of his own about everything, but could not bear to import it to any one. He lived alone. Hardly any one among us had ever been in his lodging.

This was what I read in the *Voice*.

"Every one knows that we are progressive and humanitarian and want to be on a level with Europe in this respect. But in spite of all our exertions and the efforts of our paper we are still far from maturity, as may be judged from the shocking incident which took place yesterday in the Arcade and which we predicted long ago. A foreigner arrives in the capital bringing with him a crocodile which he begins exhibiting in the Arcade. We immediately hasten to welcome a new branch of useful industry such as our powerful and varied fatherland stands in great need of. Suddenly yesterday at four o'clock in the afternoon a gentleman of exceptional stoutness enters the foreigner's shop in an intoxicated condition, pays his entrance money, and immediately without any warning leaps into the jaws of the crocodile, who was forced, of course, to swallow him, if only from an instinct of self-preservation, to avoid being crushed. Tumbling into the inside of the crocodile, the stranger at once dropped asleep. Neither the shouts of the foreign proprietor, nor the lamentations of his terrified family, nor threats to send for the police made the slightest impression. Within the crocodile was heard nothing but laughter and a promise to flay him (*sic*), though the poor mammal, compelled to swallow such a mass, was vainly shedding tears. An uninvited guest is worse than a Tartar. But in spite of the proverb the insolent visitor would not leave. We do not know how to explain such barbarous incidents which prove our lack of culture and disgrace us in the eyes of foreigners. The recklessness of the Russian temperament has found a fresh outlet. It may be asked what was the object of the uninvited visitor? A warm and comfortable abode? But there are many excellent houses in the capital with very cheap and comfortable lodgings, with the Neva water laid on, and a staircase lighted by gas, frequently with a hall-porter maintained by the proprietor. We would call our readers' attention to the barbarous treatment of domestic animals: it is difficult, of course, for the crocodile to digest such a mass all at once, and now he lies swollen out to the size of a mountain, awaiting death in insufferable agonies. In Europe persons guilty of inhumanity towards domestic animals have long been punished by law. But in spite of our European enlightenment, in spite of our European pavements, in spite of the European architecture of our houses, we are still far from shaking off our time-honoured traditions.

"Though the houses are new, the conventions are old."

And, indeed, the houses are not new, at least the staircases in them are not. We have more than once in our paper alluded to the fact that in the Petersburg Side in the house of the merchant Lukyanov the steps of the wooden staircase have decayed, fallen away, and have long been a danger for Afimya Skapidarov, a soldier's wife who works in the house, and is often obliged to go up the stairs with water or armfuls of wood. At last our predictions have come true: yesterday evening at half-past eight Afimya Skapidarov fell down with a basin of soup and broke her leg. We do not know whether Lukyanov will mend his staircase now, Russians are often wise after the event, but the victim of Russian carelessness has by now been taken to the hospital. In the same way we shall never cease to maintain that the houseporters who clear away the mud from the wooden pavement in the Viborgsky Side ought not to spatter the legs of passersby, but should throw the mud up into heaps as is done in Europe," and so on, and so on.

"What's this?" I asked in some perplexity, looking at Prohor Savvitch. "What's the meaning of it?"

"How do you mean?"

"Why, upon my word! Instead of pitying Ivan Matveitch, they pity the crocodile!"

"What of it? They have pity even for a beast, a *mammal*. We must be up to Europe, mustn't we? They have a very warm feeling for crocodiles there too. He-he-he!"

Saying this, queer old Prohor Savvitch dived into his papers and would not utter another word.

I stuffed the *Voice* and the *News-sheet* into my pocket and collected as many old copies of the newspapers as I could find for Ivan Matveitch's diversion in the evening, and though the evening was far off, yet on this occasion I slipped away from the office early to go to the Arcade and look, if only from a distance, at what was going on there, and to listen to the various remarks and currents of opinion. I foresaw that there would be a regular crush there, and turned up the collar of my coat to meet it. I somehow felt rather shy — so unaccustomed are we to publicity. But I feel that I have no right to report my own prosaic feelings when faced with this remarkable and original incident.